LAB 6

D0104983

They see the things we can't see....

WATCHERS ™

WATCHERS™

LAB 6

PETER LERANGIS

AN
APPLE
PAPERBACK

SCHOLASTIC INC.
New York Toronto London Auckland Sydney
Mexico City New Delhi Hong Kong

ISBN 0-590-11501-4

12 11 10 9 8 7 6 5 4   4/0

Printed in the U.S.A.   40
First Scholastic printing, October 1999

LAB 6

WATCHERS

Case File: 7222

Name: Samuel Hughes

Age: 13

First contact: 41.33.02

Acceptance: Yes

1

"**T**ell me why I shouldn't smash your face."

Bart Richter could hardly get the words out. His teeth were clenched, like a mouse-trap that had snapped just short of its prey.

Sam Hughes felt like the mouse.

Run.

He's crazy.

Sam knew he should have given Bart the computer class homework — just handed him a copied disk, no tricks. He should have let Bart cheat, same as always. Maybe change a line here and there so it wouldn't be too obvious.

Planting the virus was stupid.

What was I thinking? Sam asked himself.

The plan seemed foolproof at the time. It wasn't a *killer* virus. It was easy to fix. Bart would insert the disk into his computer. His files would disappear. He'd call Sam in desperation. Sam would rush over, suddenly the hero. He'd agree to retrieve the files — but only if Bart agreed to stop the cheating.

But foolproof was not the same as Bartproof.

Bart had never opened the disk. Instead, he had just handed it in.

The first person to open it had been Mr. Antonelli, the computer teacher.

And *his* files had been wiped out.

His class notes, his family finances, his e-mail, and the first seven chapters of his Great American Novel — all were gone in an instant.

By the end of the day, Bart was gone, too. From school, that is. Suspended. But only after Mr. Antonelli had yelled at him, flunked him, and threatened to sue him.

4

Which was why Sam was in the back of the Blue Mountain Mall on Friday evening, facing doom in the form of a fourteen-year-old halfback bent on vengeance.

"Mr. Antonelli's a smart guy," Sam said, backpedaling. "It's an easy virus. He — he can undelete those files, no sweat. I can tell him how, if you — "

Sam's back made contact with the brick wall. He looked to his right, toward the mall entrance, but a Dumpster blocked it from view.

Bart kept approaching. "I don't get it. What idiot would put a *virus* on his own homework?"

"It wasn't on *my* disk."

No.

Sam, you fool.

The realization slowly spread across Bart's face. "You did it to me on purpose — ?"

"I didn't think you'd hand it in — "

Bart swung. Fast.

Sam ducked, but he wasn't quick enough.

He was jolted off the ground, following the trajectory of his flying jaw. With a resounding CLANG, he slammed against the side of the Dumpster.

"Use your brain NOW, smart guy," Bart growled.

He reared his arm back again.

Sam gripped the lip of the Dumpster and pulled himself up. The smell of rotting food wafted up from inside.

He felt Bart's hand close around his calf.

"BART!"

Jamie Richter's voice.

Bart's twin sister. The lead singer in the worst garage band Sam had ever heard, Inhuman Phenomena. "The voice of a dying tomcat on a rainy night," he had said in his school newspaper review.

Maybe he'd been too harsh.

You've sabotaged one Richter. Insulted the other.

Great, Sam.

No way out of this one.

"Hulllk — " A cry for help choked in Sam's throat. He coughed out a glob of saliva.

Bart's grip loosened. "What the — ?"

Bart was stumbling backward. Wiping goo from his face. Sam's goo.

Dead.

You are dead.

"BART, YOU FATHEAD!"

Jamie's footsteps rang out. Coming closer.

Bart turned. "WHAT?" he snapped.

NOW.

Sam jumped back onto the blacktop. The impact sent a stab of pain through his already swelling jaw.

Bart spun around and lunged for him.

But Sam was gone. Running across the lot.

"Sam?" Jamie called out.

Sam darted out onto the sidewalk.

"SAM, I HAVE TO TALK TO YOU!"

Now they were both chasing him.

He ran down the hill. Toward Rio de Ratas, "River of Rats," the brownish waterway that bordered town. The river had a real name, but no one remembered it. Pollution from Blue Mountain's factories had ruined the water ages ago. Nowadays the factories stood empty and abandoned, but the look and stench of the river remained.

Just before the river was a cyclone fence. Sam squeezed through a hole, under a lopsided, sun-bleached sign that bore the faint words BLUE MOUNTAIN INDUSTRIAL PARK.

The setting sun made black holes of the

alleyways that snaked between the old brick buildings. Sam's footsteps tapped flatly against the cracked blacktop. Wary eyes glared at him as he passed makeshift shelters of old planks and cardboard boxes piled against the walls at the edges of the street-lamp light.

Where is it?

He hadn't been to the Turing-Douglas Research Labs in a long time. Not since he was a kid. But it would be a perfect hiding place.

Down Front Street, then right on Second.

The memories bubbled up through his panic. Coming to this neighborhood with his parents when he was a kid, night after night. The dank, stuffy labs where Mom and Dad told him to do his homework while they worked. The electronic equipment that loomed over him, beeping and burbling while he tried to concentrate but never could, because of that feeling, that weird feeling —

There.

As he rounded a corner he spotted the familiar rotting truck dock. The grimy, graffiti-covered tan-brick walls.

The windows of the building were dark. Maybe his mom and dad had already gone.

Just my luck.

On a normal night, they were there until midnight. Lately they'd been working on another "special government project." Sam was beginning to think there weren't really any government projects. It was an excuse to get away from him. They just liked being scientists more than being parents.

Where are they when I need them?

The front door was locked. Sam raced around to the east side of the building. In the deepening darkness, he ducked into a basement stairwell.

Something rustled from below. A small shadow scampered out of the stairwell and into the night.

Sam jumped, stifling a scream. His head banged against a cement overhang.

For a moment, everything went black. Sam crumpled to the ground.

Then he picked himself up, staggering slowly down the steps.

At the bottom, near a grime-caked basement window, he crouched and waited.

"HUGHES! I'M GOING TO GET YOU!"

Bart.

Near. Maybe thirty yards away.

The footsteps grew louder. They began circling the building, then suddenly stopped.

"AAAAAGH!" Jamie shrieked. "Rats!"

Stay put.

Just stay put.

"They're just *animals*." Bart's voice was calm, mocking.

But Jamie was already booking.

A moment later, so was Bart the Brave.

Their footsteps retreated into silence. Now the only sounds were the rustling leaves and Sam's dry, raspy breaths.

Safe.

For now, at least.

He felt his swollen jaw. It ached badly. He was bleeding a little.

Sam stood, bracing himself against the sides of the stairwell.

The bump was worse than he'd thought.

His head felt strange. As if it were expanding. As if he had to hold on to it, just to keep it intact.

And he remembered.

"Mom, can we go-o-o-o?"

"Have you finished your homework, dear?"

"I have a headache!"

"Now, Sam, why does it seem you always have a headache when you have to do homework?"

He'd had headaches a lot when he was a child. Bad ones. Just like this one — as if his head were about to explode.

It's this place. It brings out the worst in me.

As Sam climbed the stairs, a sudden throb pushed against the inside of his skull.

His knees buckled. He clutched the rusted banister.

Do. Not. Make. Noise.

Just go.

This was a bad one. A migraine, maybe. He must have really smacked the overhang hard.

Grimacing, he took another step.

The darkness gave way to a volcano of white, green, and red. As if the world had ignited.

He knew he wouldn't make it home. Not by himself.

Not even to the top of the stairs.

Help me.

HELP ME!
"Help me . . ."
Sam jumped.
For a moment the pain retracted.
The voice had come from below him.
From behind the basement window.

I'm fading.

You always knew this would happen again.

Are you prepared?

For what?

For return.

2

"Hello?" Sam's voice was barely audible.
His heart was pounding.
And his headache was gone. For now.
He knew why.
*Shock. Nature's protection. It causes pro-
duction of epinephrine, which constricts blood
vessels, shuts off pain, stimulates the heart-
beat, allows passage of electrical signals
across nerve endings. Laboratory form of epinephrine: adrenaline.*

He knew it all. He'd been reared on science.
By Dad the Artificial Intelligence Genius, by

Mom the Distinguished Professor of Neuro-biophysics.

It explained what was happening to his body.

But it didn't explain the voice.

Easy.

Calm down.

It's your imagination.

Your own thoughts.

Now use the adrenaline rush and GO.

He bolted up the stairs. The pounding resumed.

Sam stopped at the top, holding his head.

He was fooling himself to think he could make it home alone.

He had to see his mom and dad now.

Be there for me. Please be inside.

He stumbled down a steep hill toward the rear of the building, where a floodlight marked the top of a fire exit.

The door had been propped ajar with a wooden wedge. No one had bothered to close it.

Sam yanked it open and slipped inside.

He squinted against the sickly green-white

glare of the overhead fluorescents. He was in a basement corridor. Its polished wood floors and taupe-painted walls contrasted sharply with the building's depressed exterior.

LAB 10, read a sign above the nearest door.

Which offices were Mom's and Dad's? He couldn't recall. He stepped down the hallway, listening for signs of life.

"Helllllp . . ."

Sam froze.

The voice.

It was real.

And loud.

His eyes shot to the source of it. A door on the left, in the middle of the corridor.

Lab 6.

Sam began to walk toward it.

He stopped when he heard footsteps.

Two people. In the far corridor. Coming nearer.

Instinctively he backed away.

A hulking electronic instrument, covered with a canvas tarp, was propped against the wall by the stairs. An old spectrophotometer, maybe.

He ran behind it and hid.

The footsteps drew closer. Rushed. Agitated.

"I *heard* him, all the way across the building," Mrs. Hughes said.

"I'm sorry," Mr. Hughes replied.

Mom?

Dad?

Sam exhaled.

They were here after all.

Good thing they'd heard the voice. The poor dude in Lab 6 must have locked himself in.

Sam stood up. Over the top of the machine he could see his dad in front of Lab 6, fumbling for a magnetic card.

They were both so intent on opening the door, they didn't see him.

"This isn't supposed to happen," Mrs. Hughes scolded. "I told you he's too sensitive."

"My mistake," Sam's dad answered as he inserted the card in the slot. "I'll take care of it."

They pushed the door open and disappeared inside.

18

Sam slowly emerged from his hiding place and walked closer.

"He's too sensitive"?

Mr. Hughes's voice came from inside the room, muffled and soft: "Is everything all right?"

"Yes," answered the voice that Sam had heard crying for help.

It sounded young. Like someone his own age.

Sam leaned forward. The voices were hard to hear.

"What happened?" Mrs. Hughes asked.

"Someone . . . tried to get in . . . the window," the person answered.

I know that voice.

"No one's at the window now," said Mr. Hughes.

Mrs. Hughes sighed. "Probably a squirrel. This has happened before."

"I guess I should silence him, huh?"

Sam froze.

"I told you that a long time ago," Mrs. Hughes scolded. "But you never listen."

"Fine. I'll fix everything. He won't make another sound, until we need him."

What?

Sam curled down lower, into a ball.

He felt dizzy and scared.

It wasn't the headache or the pain from the bump.

It was the sound of cold, hollow tapping.

And the total silence that followed as his mom and dad left the room.

They've succeeded. After all this time.

Not quite.

So why must I prepare?

Because when they do, you must leave us.

I don't want to leave!

You're still human.

And you will forget — unless you do as we say . . .

3

A prisoner.

Mom and Dad have a prisoner in there.

Had.

HAVE. Be positive. He must be alive, right?

WHAT JUST HAPPENED?

Sam stayed hidden, listening.

They were walking away now, back down the hall, arguing in hushed voices.

Sam's head pulsed angrily. He struggled to focus.

What did Dad mean by *fix*?

Silence. Heal. Straighten out.

Kill.

They're scientists. He's a spy.

He's a political prisoner.

That's their "special government project."

No.

It was impossible. It didn't make sense.

Mom and Dad were good people, basically. They had their flaws, yes. They worked too late and ignored their son. Mom was quiet and hard to read. Dad was forgetful and eccentric; before the Turing-Douglas project, he hadn't been able to hold a job. But that was it — no malice, no evil deeds. They had kind and caring spirits.

That's what you always hear in the news whenever they catch some murderer. "We never suspected it. Such a normal, caring, kind person . . ."

Sam blocked the thought. Mom and Dad were *scientists*. All they knew was Artificial Intelligence.

AI.

Sam thought of Bart as an eight-year-old, lurching across the Hugheses' front lawn like Frankenstein's monster, screaming "AIIIII!" That was Bart's idea of clever wordplay.

But everyone else shared the same stereotype. To all the kids at school, AI meant cyborgs and robots and —

What was it that Jamie used to talk about? Morbid Jamie, who'd kill off her Barbies in "tragic accidents" and then hold funerals for them?

Humans made of spare parts, locked in dark underground lairs — that was HER idea of what happened at Turing-Douglas.

Ridiculous.

Or was it?

Sam moved into the hallway. Silently. Slowly, too, because his head couldn't withstand sudden motion.

The door to Lab 6 was shut tight. He grabbed the doorknob and tried to turn it — just in case Dad forgot to lock it. Which would be just like him.

It held fast.

Sam rapped on the door — quietly first, then louder.

"Hey," he whispered, "anyone in there?"

No response.

He leaned his shoulder against the door and pushed.

Yeow.

The pain was excruciating. In his jaw.

And in his head.

He couldn't try again. One more jolt and his brain would keep going. It would crash through the door, leaving his body to fall in a heap.

Go. Get out of here.

And do what? Get help? Tell someone? "Officer, my parents are working on an experiment with a person locked in a lab?"

Just go.

Sam ran. Down the hall. Back upstairs. Outside. He held in the pain. He knew that if he allowed the slightest sound to escape, just the slightest —

Hold . . .

It . . .

Sam.

Then he couldn't take it, he was yelling, the screams ripping through him like a buzz saw — one word, over and over and over — he didn't know what it was and didn't care, because it was like expelling a poison, as if the volume of sound would stop the agony that blinded him as he ran through empty,

26

unforgiving streets, away from the building, away away —

He rounded a corner and plunged into a dark alleyway (*home, just get me on the road to home*), his feet splashing in a rivulet of unidentifiable liquid, when he heard the other footsteps (*where?*) coming closer and tried to stop short, tried to get a grip, but he was moving too fast, and he emerged from the alley into a pale circle of street-lamp light when he collided with a dark figure.

Quickly. Begin imprinting process.

But I'm feeling stronger.

Pay attention.

Please. I belong here.

4

"AAAAGGHHHH!"

Sam bounced back. In the dim light, he saw the gaunt, severe face of his attacker.

"Jamie?"

"You made me drop my backpack!" Jamie shouted, picking up her black leather sack. "What are you yelling about?"

"You scared me."

"You were yelling *before* you saw me."

"My head . . ."

"What happened, Bart smacked you? Good.

Did he get any teeth? Maybe he knocked some sense into you."

"I — I have to go," Sam sputtered, walking away.

"That's what you think." Jamie fell in step with him. Lit from above, her cheeks seemed to have sunk inward.

A skull.

During the day she *worked* to look like that, laying on the gothic makeup — jet-black lips and eyebrows, white base.

Tonight she didn't need any of it.

"Please — " Sam began.

"Really, really stupid review," Jamie said. "Do you understand the word *style*, Sam? Or *edge*? Have you ever listened to any music after, like, the Beatles?"

"Not now, Jamie. This is not the time."

"And then you dump on my brother. So it's, like, war on the Richter family? What next? Destroy my mom's business?"

"JAMIE, WILL YOU KNOCK IT OFF? I DON'T CARE!" Sam propped himself against a wall. Yelling was bad. Yelling hurt. "Just . . . go away, okay?"

Jamie drew closer, eyeing him warily.

"You're not lying about that headache, are you?"

Sam shook his head.

Jamie pulled him away from the wall.

Sam flinched. "Look, if you're going to take me to Bart — "

"He's probably home already. He has the attention span of a fruit fly. I can't believe he actually hurt you so bad. You must have gotten him really mad. Come on."

They began to walk away from Turing-Douglas. "It wasn't just Bart," Sam said. "I hit my head. Hiding behind the lab."

"What were you doing *there*?"

"My parents work there. Remember?"

"So? I thought you never went near there. Guess I was wrong. No wonder your brain is warped."

"What's that mean?"

"You know. The germs."

"*What* germs?"

"Uh, I can't believe you don't *know* this, or maybe you're just in *denial* — but that place is, like, *full* of mutant forms and whatever. Everyone knows that. The people who work there pass all the weird stuff to their kids. In the genes."

"Thanks for telling me."

"So what happened to Kevin?"

"Kevin who?"

"Uh, hel-*lo*? The guy whose name you were just yelling?"

Sam gave her a blank look. "I don't know anybody by that name."

"Could've fooled me."

"Maybe you heard something else. I didn't say Kevin."

Jamie rolled her eyes. "I'm losing my hearing, right? That's what happens when you're in a rock band, right? 'Cause it's all just noise, anyway — "

"I never said *that* — "

"You're just like my dad. He doesn't *get* it, either. Are you sure you're not, like, forty-five years old?"

Sam took a deep breath. He caught the sweet, smoky scent of a burning fireplace from a house on Ravensburg Avenue. He and Jamie were leaving the industrial park now; the surrounding landscape was a familiar suburban silhouette.

She's helping you. Even after what you did to her.

Cut her some slack.

"Okay, I don't *know* for sure what I said," Sam confessed. "It wasn't just a headache. It was more than that — a migraine or something. Worse. Like temporary insanity. I was hearing things."

"Hearing things?" Jamie's face brightened. "Like what?"

"Voices. You know."

"Like a moaning?"

"Sort of."

"A cry for help?"

"Well . . . yeah. How — ?"

"I've heard of this," Jamie said excitedly. "They're doing human experimentation down there. Growing mutants in test tubes. Cutting people apart and pasting the pieces together — "

"Jamie, that's ridiculous."

"How do you know?"

"Don't you think my parents would tell me — ?"

"Uh, excuse me? Wake up to the twenty-first century, Sam. It's all top secret. Government projects." Jamie pulled her backpack around, reached in, and yanked out a dog-eared magazine. "Look at this."

She paused under a street lamp. Sam caught a glimpse of the title page:

Professor Phlingus's Vault of Phreakish Phenomena
for the Strong of Stomach

As Jamie leafed through, Sam saw page after page of lurid, bizarre photos — THE THREE-YEAR-OLD WITH A REAL BEARD!!!! . . . MEET MR. SPEX, A REAL FOUR-EYES!!! SAVE THIS GRAY WOLF — WAIT, IT'S A MAN!!! . . . FROM THIS PLANET? YOUR CALL!! — with sinister-looking graphics and hysterical text to match the screaming headlines.

Sam groaned. "Oh, please."

"Wait! Skip the first half. It's all stupid stuff. But look in the back — this chapter here: 'Real Scientific Phenomena Too Disturbing for the Mass Media.' It's totally necessary to *know* this. It's the future of our world. And — I'm telling you this so you'll understand, and if you laugh I'll kill you — it's also what my songs are about. It's the whole inspiration for Inhuman Phenomena."

"*This* stuff is? Circus freaks?"

"Government conspiracies. Mind control. Just read it. *Then* talk to me."

She folded up the magazine and shoved it into Sam's back pocket.

The magazing was stupid. Embarrassing.

Government conspiracies.

That was always the excuse for things people couldn't explain. Alien abductions. Epidemics. UFOs.

If in doubt, blame the government.

But you were doing it, too, Sam.

Back in the basement at Turing-Douglas. You were imagining spies and political prisoners.

Sam inhaled the smoky autumnal air. He was farther away from the lab now. He could be more rational.

No more hysteria, Sam. When you think it through, you'll realize there must be an explanation.

Epidemics are random. Weather balloons look like flying saucers. The water supply does not contain mind control drugs. And the Turing-Douglas basement doesn't have any mutant prisoners.

"You know, most of this stuff can be explained," Sam said.

"Then why is it so secret?" Jamie persisted. "Why can't your parents tell you what they do?"

"They do — well, some of it. They're working on an electronic copy of a human brain."

"*See?* That's why they have the corpses and stuff down there."

"No, Jamie. It's boring and mechanical. Something about *switches*. The brain has these nerve endings that are like on-off switches? When you think — when you feel — electricity flashes across billions of these switches in a complicated pattern. So if you re-create the patterns — "

"You make a brain."

"So that's what my parents are doing. Working on a map. Of switches."

"And?"

"And what?"

"And what else? They have to be working on something else. To explain the screaming voices — "

"Jamie — "

"Sam, don't play dumb. What you just

described — the switches — everybody knows that. I've read about it in *Professor Phlingus*. Your mom and dad haven't told you the *secret* part. They're not *allowed* to. You're not seeing the obvious."

"Which is?"

Jamie exhaled impatiently. "Okay, so they make a map. They even build a brain. Then what? How do they know it's working? Say the brain is programmed to see. It needs eyes, right? Say the brain can feel anger. How do you *know*, unless it has a mouth to tell you? It needs human parts, Sam!"

"Well, I guess you could look at it that way."

"How *else* could you look at it?"

As they walked up Sam's street, Jamie fell silent.

The brain needs a body.

("Hellllp me . . .")

Sam tried to block the memory of the voice. It still haunted him.

There had to be a way to find out more.

Sam's house was in sight now. Its gabled Victorian tower jutted over the tops of the adjacent small ranch houses.

The tower room. Mom and Dad's computer.

The tower was their home office. All their files were on the computer there. Sam wasn't allowed in, but he'd never tested the rule.

Maybe if he just wandered up there. Maybe if Dad had been his usual absentminded self and forgotten to lock it . . .

"Sam?" Jamie said. "You're quiet. Are you having a relapse?"

"Actually I'm okay now."

As they turned up Sam's front walk Jamie patted the magazine in his pocket. "Return it to me in school tomorrow. And don't let anyone else see it."

Oh, great. She has to walk me home. My neighbors have to see Ms. Skullface walking me home, tapping me on the butt —

"Fine," Sam said curtly. " 'Bye."

Jamie smiled. "Glad you feel better."

Sam felt instantly guilty for his disparaging thoughts. "Okay. Thanks, Jamie."

He turned and inserted his key in the front door.

He didn't see the shadow behind the azalea bush until the door was open.

"Now we can get started," said a deep voice. Bart's.

CHANGE OF WATCHER STATUS

Stage: 1

Origin: Earth

Current Status: Permanent

New Status: Corporeal Transfer

Return Date: Unknown

Reason: Unknown

Imprinting: Begun

5

"**B**art, look, I'm sorry." Sam backed inside the house, trying to swing the door shut. He could picture tomorrow's headlines: EIGHTH-GRADER ACCOSTED IN HIS OWN HOUSE . . . HOMEWORK SCANDAL TURNS DEADLY . . . VIRUS LEADS TO VIOLENCE. "Really. I promise I'll talk to Mr. Antonelli. I'll call him. Now. Okay?"

Bart leaped onto the porch, throwing a sidearm block to the closing door. "Too late, pal — "

"Can't you see Sam is sick, you putrid slab of beef?" Jamie yelled.

"Oh, so you two are like . . . ?" Bart raised and lowered his eyebrows.

"NO!" Sam snapped.

"What are you doing here?" Jamie demanded.

"It's not what I'm doing, it's what I'm *going* to do." Bart leveled his eyes at Sam. "May I come in?"

"Oh, that's good, Bart — trash his house," Jamie snapped sarcastically. "Sam's parents won't suspect a thing."

"They're not *here*?" Bart grinned.

Sam shot a glance at Jamie. "Thanks a lot."

Bart was already pushing his way into the living room.

"Hey!" Sam shouted.

"Don't worry, he's chicken," Jamie said.

"Where are you going?" Sam demanded, following Bart through the house.

Bart turned into the stairway and began bounding up, two steps at a time. "To find your bedroom."

"But it's — " Sam cut himself off before saying *on the first floor*.

Bart stomped through Mr. and Mrs.

Hughes's bedroom on the second floor, then headed for the guest room.

As Sam clambered up after him, Bart ran for the rickety staircase to the tower attic.

To Mom and Dad's office.

"That's not my room, Bart!" Sam called out, sprinting to the foot of the tower stairs. *"I'm not even allowed up there!"*

Bart was turning the knob.

You locked the door, right, Dad? You weren't absentminded. Not today.

The door swung open.

Sam rushed upstairs. "No! Please! It's my parents'! There's all kinds of national security stuff in there."

"Cool." Bart was already sitting at the computer, inserting a disk into the slot. "Guess they'll be upset that their son was fooling around with their stuff."

"I'll tell them — "

"Not if you value your life."

"The virus won't wipe anything out!" Sam blurted out. "It's not that sophisticated."

Bart grinned. "So why are you worried?"

Because I may be wrong.

Because even if I'm not, it'll take FOREVER to retrieve these files.

BECAUSE I WAS A FOOL TO GIVE THE DISK TO BART IN THE FIRST PLACE.

The screen was flashing now. Then a message appeared:

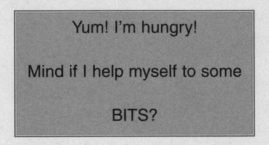

Yum! I'm hungry!

Mind if I help myself to some

BITS?

Sam blanched. *He'd* written that. It had been meant for Bart.

Code streamed across the screen — warning signs and total gibberish.

"JA-A-A-AMIIEEEEE!" Sam yelled.

Jamie came running up the stairs. "What's he doing?"

"Stop him!" Sam said. "He won't smash YOUR face in!"

They both lunged for Bart. They grabbed his shoulders and pulled.

He rolled back on the wooden floor, grinning, as another message popped onto the screen:

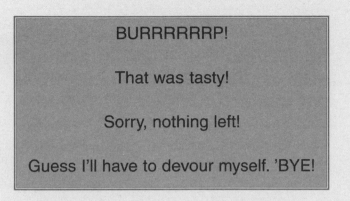

BURRRRRRP!

That was tasty!

Sorry, nothing left!

Guess I'll have to devour myself. 'BYE!

As the screen went black, Bart howled with laughter. "Guess we're even now, huh?"

"You are slime," Jamie hissed.

Sam slumped over the desk. "My parents will kill me."

With a big yawn, Bart stood up and walked toward the door. "Then I guess that'll save me the dirty work."

Let us begin.

Can't I refuse — and just stay here?

You will interfere with their affairs.

They're interfering with ours.

But we serve them.

Please. It is simple. We direct the question to your long-term memory quadrant.

Then you reply.

WE ARE CALLED . . .

I repeat. WE ARE CALLED . . .

Watchers . . .

6

```
UNDELETING . . .

□ BRAIN-SIZE MAP . . .

□ CEREBRAL NEPHRITIC SWITCH CIRCUITRY . . .

□ SYNTHETIC EPITHELIAL MATERIAL . . .
```

Sam's fingers flew over the keyboard. He didn't know what any of the file names meant. But they were all coming back. All of them.

"Done yet?" Jamie's voice called from behind him.

"Go home," Sam grumbled.

"Ingrate."

Thump.

The car door.

In the driveway.

Sam bolted up from the chair. He ran to the tower room's only window. It was almost opaque with dust, but he could make out the shapes of his parents, climbing out of their car.

He spun around and noticed Jamie for the first time since he'd started undeleting files. She was sitting on the floor, rummaging through papers in a file cabinet. She wore Mrs. Hughes's old porkpie hat and a tie-dye shirt that had been hanging on the coatrack for ages, cinched with a thick black leather belt Sam had never seen before. "JAMIE, PUT THAT STUFF AWAY AND GET OUT OF HERE!"

No time to argue. Sam sprinted downstairs, through the house, and outside.

His parents were trudging up the front lawn.

"HI, guys!" Sam said. "How's it GOING?" *Too loud. Don't try too hard.*

"Tired," his dad said. "It's been a long week."

Mrs. Hughes was looking at his jaw. "Sam, were you in a fight?"

"I fell . . . in gym."

"You fell on your jaw?" Mr. Hughes asked.

"Sounds like a cranial nerve problem," Mrs. Hughes said.

"No! I'm okay," Sam insisted. "Really."

"Well, maybe you're overtired," Mrs. Hughes said. "I'm heading right to bed. You should, too."

"Bed?" Sam stood in front of them. His eyes darted up toward the tower window, which emitted a soft glow. "Wait! Don't go in! I mean, it's a perfect night. I was just going to take a walk. Want to come? We haven't had a family walk in a long time."

"We've never had family walks," Mrs. Hughes said.

Slam.

Sam spun around. Jamie was walking out of the house. No hat. No tie-dye shirt. Her black bangs fell across her eyes as she muttered hello.

"Jamie Richter?" said Mrs. Hughes.

Mr. Hughes raised an eyebrow to Sam. An *I-didn't-know-you-were-interested-in-girls* eyebrow.

"We were . . . doing homework," Sam improvised.

"Yeah," said Jamie unconvincingly.

"Ooooh, I love that *belt*," Mrs. Hughes said. "I had one just like it, years ago."

The belt. She HAD to forget to put back one thing. . . .

Jamie looked down, befuddled.

"Well, see you, Jamie!" Sam blurted out, heading into the house. "Come on, Mom and Dad!"

"No family walk, Sam?" Mr. Hughes gave his wife a knowing grin.

Mrs. Hughes gently pulled Sam back. "Why don't you give your friend a proper good-bye?"

"What — well, I — "

"Don't be too long," Mrs. Hughes sang, walking into the house with her husband.

As the front door shut behind them, Jamie burst out laughing. "They think we're — you and me — "

"THIS ISN'T FUNNY!" Sam snapped. "Half

54

their files are still missing — and you just stole Mom's belt!"

"Get a life, Sam," Jamie said, walking away.

Sam noticed her backpack was open. "Wait a minute. What else do you have in there?"

Jamie spun around. "Nothing."

"Show me."

"It's none of your business."

"Your next concert gig is Sunday, right? I'm thinking of coming, with my pen and pad."

Jamie glowered at him. Sullenly she pulled around her backpack and held it open.

Sam yanked out the tie-dye shirt. A white fright wig left over from some Halloween. A black grease pencil. A marble composition notebook.

"They're not going to *miss* any of it," Jamie said.

But Sam wasn't listening.

He held the notebook slantways, letting the porch light illuminate the cover. Written across the front label, in his dad's scrawly handwriting, was a name.

Kevin Hughes.

WE ARE . . .

Council and Protector of the Realities.

WE LIVE IN . . .

The Tenth Oscillation, encompassing the nine dimensions within.

WHICH INCLUDE . . .

Parallel-time worlds, travel holes along the space-time continuum.

Hurry . . .

1

"You wrote this, didn't you?" Sam said.

Jamie peered over his shoulder at the scribble. "No way. Who's Renin Hugges?"

"Kevin Hughes," Sam said.

"So you *do* know a Kevin — and he's *related* to you?"

"No!"

Sam leafed through the book. The first page was dated 9/28 — yesterday's date.

He tried to decipher what was under it:

Lab 6

Circuits: 111100 1110 - 101111011   OK

Neurotransmitter calibration: COMPLETE
                                    (FINALLY!)

Transport readiness: ✓

Closet

Epithelial elasticity: OK

Fluid temperature simulation: 98.2°F

Respiratory apparatus: ✓

Est. time until completion: 1 month

"What language is that?" Jamie asked.

"My dad's English," Sam replied.

"What's it say?"

"How should I know? Nobody can read his writing."

Sam flipped past the first page. The rest of the book was empty.

"Maybe your dad's real name is Kevin," Jamie said. "And he never told you."

"That's totally stupid."

"Or he's leading a double life — "

"As a scientist who writes up his experiments in composition notebooks? That's the same as his first life."

"Or maybe 'Kevin Hughes' isn't your dad. It's a long-lost cousin."

"And Dad's doing an experiment on him?"

Jamie thought for a moment. "Kevin's not too bright. He's embarrassed to go public. Your dad's trying to give him some artificial intelligence."

Sam slapped his head in a mock *aha!* "And he's locked in Lab 6 — crying for help! *That's* who I heard."

"Sam, you may be on to something," Jamie said.

Stupid.

Totally birdbrained.

As bad as her brother.

"It was a joke, Jamie — "

"Maybe you weren't so whacked out as you thought," Jamie said. "You really heard the voice."

"I didn't. I had a migraine."

"You were shouting his name. You were shouting 'Kevin.' Somehow you knew his secret identity!"

"Oh? And how would that be?"

"I don't know. People recover memories. Especially when they're in pain." Jamie pointed to the magazine in Sam's pocket. "Look in there. One guy was abducted to a planet where he lived for eleven years with alien shepherds who wiped out his memory, and — "

"Great, Jamie. Very interesting. Can I go to bed now?"

Jamie gave him a withering look. "Don't forget your warm milk and cookies."

As she turned away, Sam dropped the composition notebook into his shirt and went inside.

The house was still. Mr. and Mrs. Hughes were already upstairs.

Please please not the tower room.

No. They wouldn't have. They were too tired. They didn't usually go up there after work anyway. Just weekends and early mornings.

Sam tiptoed to his room. He could hear his parents upstairs, getting ready for bed. If he went to the tower room now, they'd hear the old steps creaking.

Closing his bedroom door, Sam carefully removed the notebook and hid it under his mattress. He jumped when he heard a door close, but it was the second-floor bathroom. He could hear his dad yawning from within.

Sam went to wash up in his own bathroom. As he passed the kitchen, he caught a glimpse of the stove clock, glowing in the darkness — 11:17.

His stomach gave a low growl. He realized he hadn't eaten dinner. He was starving.

He detoured to the fridge and pulled it open.

Upstairs his dad was gargling now. To the tune of "If I Were a Rich Man."

Singing. As if nothing strange had happened tonight. Just another day at work.

Had anything strange happened?

What exactly had Sam seen?

What had he heard?

A voice calling for help.

Mom and Dad running down the hallway.

Then Sam had ducked behind the machine. He'd heard Mom and Dad talking to —

To whom?

The prisoner?

Earlier, the idea had seemed to make so much sense.

But with that headache, blue elephants tap-dancing through the hallways would have seemed possible.

Think, Sam.

What if someone at the lab had accidentally locked himself in — a young scientist, a researcher, a maintenance worker? The guy had heard Sam outside and cried for help. Mom and Dad heard the voice and unlocked the door.

The strange conversation — all that stuff about silencing the guy and his being "too sensitive" — Sam could have heard it wrong. The voices had been muffled and distant.

They were down the hall. In a room. Separated from me by fifteen yards and a thick wall.

It also could have been a joke — his mom and dad pretending to be heavies, to tease the guy. They had that nerdy sense of humor.

Okay, so they released him and went on with their business. Simple.

But they hadn't left with anyone. They had walked away together, alone.

Or had they?

Maybe not. Sam hadn't seen them. He had been hiding behind the machine. He'd only *heard* them.

There could have been three sets of footsteps. Mom, Dad, and the guy, off to resume work.

With a sigh, Sam pulled out from the fridge a white cardboard container of Chinese leftovers. He put it on the table and opened it.

Stir-fried chicken.

With hair.

Sam nearly gagged. The greenish-white

mold made the chicken look like some bizarre science experiment.

Typical.

Food tended to sit unnoticed for weeks.

Like everything else in the house.

Sam tossed the food in the trash.

What was so important that they had to stay so late all the time? Did it have to do with that notebook? What was that notebook all about anyway?

Who is Kevin?

"Sam?"

His mom's voice startled Sam. "Yeah?"

"What's up, sweetie?" she said, walking into the kitchen. "Insomnia?"

"Yeah." Sam managed a wan smile. "Headache. You know. No big deal."

"May have been caused by that fall."

"Fall?"

"In gym? When you hurt your jaw?"

"Oh, *that* fall."

Mrs. Hughes reached into the fridge and pulled out some milk.

"Smell it first, okay?" Sam warned.

"We bought this one yesterday." As she poured a couple of glasses, she looked lost in thought. "So, when did the headache start, Sam?"

"Uh . . . after school."

"Big one?"

"I guess."

"This isn't like you. You never have headaches anymore." As Mom set the two milk glasses on the table, she had that *you're-not-telling-me-the-whole-story* look on her face. "Sam, where did you go after school today?"

He assembled a story quickly. "My jaw? It wasn't a fall in gym. Bart and I got into this fight. I ran away. But he chased me all the way into the old industrial zone — "

"So you were near Turing-Douglas? And you didn't come in to see us?"

"Well, I — I was going to. But the door was locked. So . . . I hid from Bart . . . and then I left."

"But you were near the building — and that's when you had this headache?"

"Exactly!"

"Like, hiding near one of the basement windows or something?"

Sam gulped. "Yes."

His mom nodded slowly and sipped her milk. "Sam, do you remember when you were a kid, and you had these strange feelings at Turing-Douglas — back when we started working on the project?"

Sam nodded. "I hated being there."

"You said you felt like someone else was inside you, and he wanted to get out."

"I was a kid, Mom — "

"Did this headache feel like that?"

"I guess."

What is she getting at?

Something was up. Mom's voice was edgy.

"Mom? Is something wrong? Am I . . . allergic to something at Turing-Douglas?"

"Allergic?"

"Like . . . I don't know, mutant germs or something?"

"Turing-Douglas is not an epidemiology lab," Mom said, getting up from the table. "No germ research, just computers. I'm sure it's nothing serious. You just need sleep. And frankly, so do your father and I."

She put her glass in the sink and headed upstairs.

68

Sam lasted a while longer, then went to his room.

He tried not to think of the day's events. He climbed into bed.

The milk had had no effect. He was wired.

He tried to count sheep. He tried to look at a spot on the wall until his eyes closed. When none of that worked, he tried the killer method: devising computer code in his sleep. The ultimate self-boredom technique.

Click.

His parents' bedroom door opened.

Sam's body tensed.

Dad was walking up to the tower room. Sam recognized the heaviness of the step, even though Dad was tiptoeing.

The light.

Had Jamie left it on?

The notebook.

It was still under Sam's mattress.

Sam broke into a sweat. What if Dad looked for the notebook and realized it wasn't there?

What if the Undelete utility's exit screen was on? What if it hadn't worked? What if some of Dad's files were still missing?

Did I get them all back?

Sam hadn't double-checked.

Now he could hear thumping from upstairs.

Dad was heading down again, walking toward Sam's room.

His hand turned the doorknob.

Sam quickly shut his eyes, still lying on his back.

He saw what happened and he's coming to yell at me.

Dad was making as little noise as possible, tiptoeing across the room. But not toward Sam.

The closet door opened. Sam heard the sliding and clacking of wire hangers.

Carefully he let his eyes open. Only to a slit.

Dad was slipping back out through Sam's door. He was holding a plaid flannel shirt that Sam hadn't worn in months.

On tiptoe, Dad headed down the hall.

A moment of silence, and then the front door opened and closed.

Sam slipped out of bed. Staying low, he moved to the window and peeked over.

His dad was climbing into the car. Rushing. Shoving a briefcase inside. Suddenly he looked to Sam's room.

Sam ducked.

A moment later, he heard the car roar off into the night.

OUR MISSION IS . . .

Where is he?

We've lost him.

8

"**H**ellllp me . . ."

The voice. Again.

I'm back in time. Hiding in the stairwell. Bart is somewhere close by. Losing my trail.

(YOU FELL ASLEEP. YOU'RE DREAM-ING. THIS IS NOT REAL.)

I feel it again.

The headache. The FEELING —

Something's inside me.

Pushing. Trying to get out.

GO. THERE'S NOT ENOUGH ROOM HERE.

(Wake up, Sam. WAKE UP.)

"He-e-e-elllllp!"

The voice has moved.

MOVED? HOW? WHERE?

It's not behind the basement window anymore.

It's outside.

In the darkness.

In the streets outside Turing-Douglas.

I stand up. I have to follow it.

I have to find out who it is.

(NO!)

My legs are weak. Loose and elastic.

I hold on to the banister and somehow make it to the top of the stairwell.

I don't know WHY I want to follow the voice. I don't know why I'm not running away (BECAUSE YOU'RE A FOOL), but I have to.

The feeling is strengthening. I can barely put one foot in front of the other.

"He-e-e-elllllp me . . ."

The voice is beckoning me further into the alleyways (IT'S A TRAP), the buildings around me are swelling and contracting like big, dark jellyfish — and the eyes, the eyes are watching, piercing the darkness, but I follow

76

the street maze and then I'm at the gate and suddenly I'm walking toward home.

But the voice is still with me. I sense it.

(TURN AWAY OR YOU'LL BE SORRY!)

I realize my legs aren't moving. They're locked. I'm being pulled now. I'm floating, my entire body rigid and helpless.

"WHO ARE YOU?"

I'm shouting but somehow the words stay inside my head as I sail through the town . . . through my neighborhood . . .

Then I'm in front of my house. And I suddenly turn up the walkway.

The voice is calling from inside.

"HE-E-E-ELLLLP!"

It's deafening.

It's beyond sound.

It's a total-body sensation. As if someone is twanging a taut string that runs from my head to my ankles.

But I keep going. Because I can't stop myself.

I need to see who's calling me. The voice has something to do with the feeling in my head. If I find who's yelling, maybe the feeling will stop.

I'm in the house now. Mom and Dad are nowhere to be seen. The shouting has saturated the air; it's in the walls, making everything vibrate. And soon it's in me, too, and now I'm calling for help — my voice joining the other — as I reach the bottom of the stairs.

(NO)

The voice is coming from this floor.

From my room.

(NO — STAY AWAY!)

I can't fight it. The sound itself is moving me — right to my door, making my hand reach out to the knob.

I try to pull back but it's no use. It is — he is — (I AM) calling and I can't resist.

I turn the knob.

The door whooshes open and slams against the wall. Inside, the room is bathed in a harsh white light. A stranger sits at my desk, his back to me.

I panic. Who is he? Is he the one? Is he shouting for help? I can't tell. But I CAN see that he's wearing my flannel shirt, the one that Dad took. At first I think it's Bart — he's found Dad, stolen his keys and my shirt, and broken into the house — but no, it's not Bart,

I can tell, it's someone else, someone familiar, and I hover in the air, smothered and battered by the sound (HE-E-ELLLPPP!) as

> *he*
> *starts*
> *to*
> *turn.*

I can't close my eyes I see his profile and he IS yelling OR IS HE? no the sound is coming from ME now and it's not "Help!" I'm not shouting for help anymore it's a different word it's a name (his name) it's

> *"KE-E-E-EVINNN!"*

And now he's turned around fully.
(STOP!)
There's no question now.
I know who it is.
I've known him all along.

What is he doing?

He'll come back.

Unless he's caught. And then we'll lose him forever.

9

Sam was jolted awake.

The harsh white light was gone, the room silent.

Everything seemed wrapped in haze.

WHO?

Who was it?

The vision was fading. Or was it?

Sam tried to focus on the figure across the room. At his desk.

He's still there.

He was standing now. Staring at Sam.

Approaching.

Sam scrambled to leave, but his feet were tangled in the bedsheets.

A pair of hands grabbed him firmly.

Mom's hands. She was crouched at the side of his bed.

"Sweetie, it's okay," she said. "You were dreaming."

Sam blinked. The room — and the figure — sharpened.

Dad.

It's just Dad.

Sam's desk had been cleared off. On it was a laptop he'd never seen in the house before. It was attached on one side to a towering machine, on the other to a wrinkled, leather-like object in his dad's hands.

"Are you okay, pal?" his father asked.

Sam's breathing was fast and painful. His throat felt raw, as if it had been scraped with a barbecue brush. "Yeah."

"Must have been a bad one," his mom said.

Sam nodded. "It . . . was so real."

"The brain can do that."

"Switches," his dad said with a soft smile. "Remember, that's all it is."

"What's that?" Sam asked, nodding toward the thing in his dad's hand.

"Just a prototype," he explained.

"Of *what*?"

Mr. Hughes began unfolding the object. It was concave, like a skullcap. Small electrodes protruded from the top, connected by wires to the machine.

"Please put this on," he said calmly.

Sam fought back the words — Jamie's words, the words in his fears and dreams (*experiments . . . mutants . . . prisoners in lab rooms . . . brain tampering . . .*)

STOP.

He breathed slowly, calming his still-panicked thoughts.

They are my parents.

"Why, Dad?" he asked.

"It may make you feel better," Mrs. Hughes said.

" 'May'?"

"Like I said, it's a prototype," Mr. Hughes replied. "It may do nothing. But it can't possibly hurt."

"I feel fine now!"

His mother leaned in and stroked the back of his head. "You were having that feeling, weren't you? The one you sometimes get at Turing-Douglas?"

"It was a *dream*, Mom. Really — "

"You were yelling out a name." Mr. Hughes looked at him levelly. "Do you know what it was?"

"Kevin . . ." Sam murmured.

"Yes," Mrs. Hughes said, almost under her breath.

"Who is that, Mom? Why was the name on the — ?"

You can't mention the notebook!

Sam cut himself off. The notebook was still under his bed.

His dad was at the desk again. With a flick of a switch, he turned on the laptop. The screen glowed with four graphs, all flat.

GRRRRONNNNG!

The feeling rushed back.

Like an injection of hot air into Sam's head.

"IT HURTS, DAD! DON'T DO THAT!" Sam pleaded.

"John . . ." said Mrs. Hughes anxiously.

But Sam's dad was placing the cap on him.

They're my parents.

They love me.

The graphs on the monitor instantly sprang to life — jagged, pulsating, and violent-looking.

Sam felt his eyes bulge. He felt warm spots of perspiration on his upper lip.

"WHY . . . ARE . . . YOU DOING . . . THIS?"

This isn't HELPING me. It's making everything worse, and it's DAD — Dad's idea, he doesn't know what he's doing, THAT'S why he was fired from those other jobs.

Sam reached up to pull off the cap. But he was losing balance, losing consciousness, and his fingers felt dead.

He looked desperately at his mom. "Can . . . you . . . ?"

Swallowing hard, she glanced at her husband, confusion playing across her tight, inscrutable features.

Then she reached out to Sam.

And held the cap down.

At that moment, Sam knew.

He knew that he had seen something he wasn't supposed to see.

He had witnessed the secret.

The government secret.

Do they know the risk they're taking?

They're his parents. Few risks are too big.

10

Gone.

It was gone.

The feeling had left him as suddenly as it had come.

The graphs were still jumping, but Sam was calm again.

Clear-eyed.

Mom was a mess. Wet-faced and haggard.

Dad didn't look too terrific, either. He was wide-eyed and pale, as if he'd just seen a purple horn sprout from Sam's forehead.

"I thought — you didn't — " Sam was giddy with relief. He flopped back onto his bed. "Whoa, that's some machine."

Normal.

My fingers — my eyes — my head — they feel totally normal.

Mom's jaw dropped open. "Oh my god," she whispered. "Oh my god."

Sam reached upward to remove the cap. "Can I?"

"It . . . works," his dad murmured.

Sam took that for a yes. He pulled the cap from his head. "Thanks. What's this thing called?"

"A transpatheter," his mom said, her face slowly brightening.

Dad was carefully examining the screen. He was rocking from foot to foot, practically dancing. "The neurotransmitters functioned. The circuitry was flawless."

"What does that mean?" Sam tried.

His mom ignored him. "Dendritic action?"

"Point five nanoseconds average," his dad answered.

"Storage?"

"Four million megagigs with cache to spare!"

They fell into each other's arms, giggling.

Giggling!

"What? Are we going to get rich now?" Sam asked.

They both turned to face him, as if just noticing he was in the room. Then, with big smiles, they pulled him into a three-way hug. "Richer than you can imagine," his mom said.

Sam wrapped his arms around them and squeezed.

He was strong again, clearheaded. His parents were happy.

It felt good to be together. Really good.

But something wasn't right. They were happy about the *machine*. They were happy about being rich.

He would have liked a little more concern for himself.

Don't be greedy, Sam. Take what you can get.

They've been working on this forever. Give them some credit.

"So it's some kind of medical thing?" Sam asked. "Like, stronger than aspirin without the side effects?"

Dad threw back his head, laughing. "More than that. Sam, you know what we've said all along about the human brain — "

"It's all switches," Sam said, repeating the mantra he'd heard almost as often as *Watch for traffic when you cross the street.* "Like, little electrical circuits between the nerves."

"Billions of them," his mom explained. "Every moment — every tiny feeling you experience, every thought you have — is a certain sequence of those switches, turning on and off."

"This machine," his dad said, "in essence, has those switches — "

"You mean, you've done it!" Sam asked. "You've created a real brain?"

"No," Mrs. Hughes replied. "Not a brain. Just a transpatheter — a shell. All set up to *recognize* and *receive* the various circuits of the human brain."

"It doesn't have the capacity to experience the feelings itself," Sam's dad added. "It has to wait for a signal — then uploads and stores it."

"So that headache I was having — "

Sam's mom was grinning. "It wasn't a headache, Sam. It was more than that, wasn't it?"

Much more.

Unbelievably more.

Even thinking about it hurt. "Like another person inside me . . ."

"A whole other boy," his mom agreed, "trapped inside — with emotions so strong that you feel you're going to explode."

"It's what you used to tell us years ago," Mr. Hughes said. "But now those feelings are gone, Sam. Into the transpatheter. All those awful emotions."

The graphs were still going wild.

"Like . . . uploading a part of myself," Sam whispered.

His mom put her arm around his shoulder. "You could say that."

"Then what?" Sam asked. "What happens to the emotions?"

His dad looked confused. "Well . . . they become electricity."

"But my emotions are electricity, too," Sam retorted. "And the electrical patterns cause me to *feel* a certain way. So if the machine is identical to my brain — wouldn't *it* feel, too, just like a real person?"

"To be a real person, it would need the means of expression and experience," Mr. Hughes said. "Eyes to see, ears to hear — "

"But how do you know?" Sam pressed on. "How do you *know* a machine can't feel it all inside?"

His parents exchanged a long glance.

Finally his dad said, "We don't."

Sam noticed the smell of microwaved left-overs as he stepped out of the shower. Walking to his room, he heard his parents in the kitchen, jabbering a mile a minute.

Sam wasn't often awake during their midnight snacks.

Well, 2:37 A.M. snack, to be precise. That was the time glowing on his bedroom alarm clock.

He was tired. Bone tired. The shower had

soothed him, making him realize how tense he'd been.

He'd needed that shower after the experience with the transpatheter. It had left him feeling sweaty.

Drained, too. Literally.

Whatever had been inside him was gone. His head felt totally clear.

How?

The transpatheter seemed like hocus-pocus. Like something out of *Professor Phlingus*. In theory it made sense, but if he hadn't seen it — if someone had tried to describe it to him . . .

Don't think about it now.

Sleep.

He put on a clean pair of pajamas and slid into bed.

As his eyes shut, he noticed his clothes heaped on the floor. Jamie's magazine stuck out of his pants pocket.

He made a mental note to return that to her. Not to mention —

The notebook.

Zing. Sam was awake again. He sat up and

pulled the composition notebook from under his mattress. Walking to his door, he peeked down the hallway.

Mom and Dad were out of sight, still deep into their conversation in the kitchen.

Quietly, Sam went up to the tower room.

The computer was on, the screensaver's wildly moving geometric designs casting a flickery glow over the room. Sam walked gingerly to the file cabinet and pulled open the top drawer.

He noticed the name KEVIN on a file-folder tab.

Sam eagerly pulled out the folder and opened it.

Empty.

Had the notebook been the only thing in it? One notebook with one page of writing?

He slipped the notebook in and riffled through the other file tabs. The names were all scientific words, totally baffling.

There has to be more. Somewhere.

He softly closed the file drawer and turned to the computer.

A peek wouldn't hurt. Probably all scientific gibberish anyway.

Sam sneaked over to the desk, sat down, and moved the mouse.

The screensaver disappeared, replaced by a message:

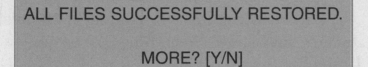

ALL FILES SUCCESSFULLY RESTORED.

MORE? [Y/N]

Sam let out a quiet sigh of relief.

He pressed N, then ran a system-wide search on the name "Kevin."

"Sam?" his mother's voice called from two floors below.

Panic.

Sam aborted the search. The screen returned to its normal state — just the way it had been before Bart had found it.

They would never know.

Sam sped down to the second floor. "Yeah?"

"Are you hungry?"

"No, thanks," Sam called when he reached the first floor. "I'm going to sleep."

"Okay. 'Night!"

" 'Night."

He hopped into bed. Finally. But instead of dozing off he lay there, staring upward, eyes wide. His heart raced.

Insomnia twice in one night. Just great.

He grabbed the nearest reading material. Jamie's magazine. Something humorous to loosen him up.

But it wasn't funny. The pictures of freakish people and animals were cheesy. Half the pictures looked doctored. It seemed wrong to ogle the others.

He was about to close it when he saw the last section, the one Jamie wanted him to read — "Real Scientific Phenomena Too Disturbing for the Mass Media."

He leafed through the alien abductions (the usual grainy photos and hysterical testimony), an article called "Return from Death: They Saw the White Light and Lived to Tell," and "The True Story of the Man Who Used Ninety-One Percent of His Brain, While the Rest of Us Use Only Fifteen!"

Junk.

Next came "Twins: The Shocking Truth of Midge and Madge, Separated at Birth and Raised in Two Different Families, Total Strangers Who Finally Meet at Age 32 and Are ABSOLUTELY IDENTICAL!!!"

Each married on the same day in the same year . . . husbands have same first name and same interests . . . each had a best friend who died in a car accident . . . both had same favorite color, same favorite song, bought same kind of house on identically named streets in two different towns.

Now that was cool.

As Sam read, he heard his mother and father clomp silently upstairs. He heard the gentle rumble of their voices, a few minutes of TV, then silence.

The whole world asleep but me.

With a yawn, Sam turned to the last page of the article. There, in a box at the bottom of the page, was a small piece entitled "Twin Tidbits."

Under the title was a close-up photo of a man's outstretched palm. He was holding a strange-looking dark clump.

Sam read the paragraph below it:

> **Absorbing mystery:** Dr. Harold Crenshaw holds a teratoma, a tumor removed from the body of Diana, a newborn at an Illinois hospital. An ultrasound scan early in the mother's pregnancy revealed twins — but soon after, one of the pair seemed to vanish. Diana was born alone. The tumor, although benign, contained bits of hair and skin and tiny remnants of what Dr. Crenshaw believes are fingernails. What happened to Diana's twin? According to Dr. Crenshaw, "Teratomas like this have been documented throughout history. It is thought that one member of the twin pair simply *absorbs* the other."

Gross.

But too bad it didn't happen to Jamie. Bart would have been a great little teratoma.

Sam smiled. The magazine had done the trick. His eyes were drooping.

No more nightmares tonight, Sam.

No more floating through streets.

No more haunted voices in your brain.

No more ghoulish scenes in your bedroom.

Sam drifted off, thinking gratefully of the strange machine that had helped him so much, and of the ludicrous ideas he had had about the voice in the basement . . .

The transpatheter took care of everything, took old Kevin away . . .

Sam's eyes sprang open.

He practically leaped out of bed.

It can't be . . .

All his thoughts were coming together in a new way.

The feeling . . .

The sense that two people were inside . . .

Midge and Madge — the connection that lasted over a lifetime, across a continent . . .

Sam rushed out of his room. Treading softly, he sneaked to the kitchen.

He tore open the phone book, found the number for Richter, and tapped it out on the phone's keypad.

"Yo."

"Jamie? Did I wake you?"

"No. Who is this?"

"Sam. Listen — "

"Do you know what time it is? Doesn't anyone sleep at your house?"

"Yeah, my parents. Meet me at the corner of Webster and Elm."

"Now? I'm practicing!"

"Take a break."

"Sam, I'm hanging up. If you call me like this again, I will kill you."

"Five minutes."

Click.

Sorry I left. But I may get this to work.

You can't. You have an obligation —

We must continue.

But I may not need to.

A safety precaution. In case we lose you. Now. OUR MISSION IS . . .

11

"This better be worth it." Jamie was livid. Sam could tell, even if he couldn't see her face in the darkness as she jogged up the street. "It's, like, four o'clock A.M."

"Three forty-five," Sam said, turning down Webster Avenue. "Just follow me."

"Where are we going?"

"To Turing-Douglas."

"WHAT? Give me one good reason I should follow you."

"I'm reviewing your next concert."

"That's a good reason." Jamie fell into step beside him.

"Jamie," Sam said firmly, "the voice I heard in the window — the voice from Lab Six — it was *my* voice. That's why it sounded familiar."

"What?"

"You believed I heard a prisoner, remember?"

"Yes."

"And you thought the prisoner was this . . . *Kevin*."

"A theory."

"Well, Kevin does exist, Jamie. He's the prisoner. And he's my twin."

She was staring at him.

Dumbfounded.

"Sam, if you're having, like, a breakdown or something, can you do it at home?"

Show her.

Sam ducked under a street lamp and pulled his shirt down, revealing a scar near his collarbone. "Look at this."

"I'm going, Sam . . ."

"The mark, Jamie! It's from an operation I

had when I was a baby. The doctors removed a growth."

"You sure they didn't remove a little something from between your ears?"

"Read this." Sam pulled out the *Professor Phlingus* magazine, open to the twin article. He handed it to her.

Jamie's eyes narrowed as she read it. "Your growth was . . . this thing? A teratoma?"

"I don't know for sure. My parents never talked about it much. They just said it was benign."

"Did they *tell* you that they'd been expecting twins?"

"No."

"So what makes you think — ?"

"Put yourself in their shoes, Jamie. The doctor says you're expecting twins. But it doesn't happen. You have one healthy boy. How will he feel if you tell him the truth? You're a twin — how would *you* have felt if you'd done that to Bart? Guilty, probably. Lonely, at least. So they hid it from me."

"So you think you *absorbed* him — "

"Those headaches — they were more than that. I felt as if two people were crowded in my brain — "

Jamie backed away. "This is weird, Sam. Even for me — "

"He stayed inside me, Jamie. All these years. I saw him in a dream tonight. He was sitting at my desk. He looked exactly like me. And I couldn't stop yelling the name Kevin. When I woke up, my parents were by my bed. They had this machine — they've been working on it for years. It can upload emotions from a human into brain circuitry. They used it on me, and the feeling disappeared. Everything was transferred out. Kevin was gone, and I was still there."

Jamie burst out laughing. "But that's ridiculous, Sam."

"Any more ridiculous than the other things in *Professor Phlingus*?"

"Hello? One major logical problem — if you absorbed him, then he's gone. If he's gone, how on earth could he be calling you from a basement window?"

"That's what I don't know! But he *did*. Maybe a part of him survived. But I have some of his brain circuitry. That would explain the transpatheter. Maybe Mom and Dad are trying to construct the rest of him — "

"Sam, that is disgusting!"

"Why would he be calling for help? Maybe he doesn't have the ability to move on his own."

"Listen to yourself. Do you really believe your parents would keep this — whatever it is, this *thing* — all locked up in the basement of a big lab for almost fourteen years, without anybody ever finding out? Do you realize how that sounds?"

Stupid.

Gruesome.

But possible.

They were scientists.

They had one child who was born healthy. Another who wasn't. For some reason, they had to keep the child hidden. Maybe they needed to protect him. Maybe he couldn't live outside the lab.

So they held on to him. They held out hope the only way they could. They waited.

Until the technology could catch up to that hope.

If you thought about it, they had no other choice. They *had* to try.

They were parents.

"I was hoping you'd understand," Sam said. "But if you don't, that's cool. Totally cool."

He turned away and began walking. As he rounded the corner, Turing-Douglas came into sight. The building was dark. Only the hum of the basement generator gave any hint that the place was different from the hulking shells around it.

Jamie's footsteps pattered up behind him. "Wait, Sam."

"Go away," Sam said resolutely.

"You need me."

"I can do this myself."

Jamie pulled a small stack of magnetic cards out of her pocket. "Not without these."

Sam stopped. The cards were marked T-D: UNAUTHORIZED USE STRICTLY PROHIBITED BY LAW and stamped with his parents' names.

"What the — "

"They were way in the back of a file cabinet drawer." Jamie shrugged. "Spares, I guess. I was going to return them, but you pitched a hissy fit in front of your house — "

"You stole them."

"You need them."

Grab them. Now.

Before you have a chance to think.

Sam took the cards and continued toward the building. Jamie followed close behind.

He braced himself for the headache to come back. But it didn't. He felt fine.

The rear door was still ajar. Sam pushed it open and stepped into the harsh light of the basement corridor.

"I don't hear anything," Jamie whispered.

"Ssshhh." Sam tiptoed down the hallway, reading the signs on the doors.

LAB 6.

His hands shook. He fumbled the cards.

Jamie took them from him and studied the fine print. She inserted one of them in the slot.

The little red indicator light turned to green. Jamie pushed.

The door swung open.

Blackness stared back at them, punctuated by tiny lights on the walls and on a console in the center of the room.

Sam stepped inside. A low thrumming

sound came from the console. He could see small backlit graphs, all trailing symmetrical sine waves. Squinting to adjust to the darkness, he felt along the door for a light switch.

Click.

Behind them, the door slammed shut.

"Jamie?" he whispered.

"Sorry," she whispered back. "There's so much *stuff* here. Where's the — "

"Da-a-ad?"

The voice made them both jump.

It was small. Muffled.

Sam's voice.

OUR MISSION IS . . .

Uh . . . to — to increase our ranks. To find those whose minds have not yet closed to the possibilities —

BECAUSE . . .

All are capable, but few are qualified.

OUR GREATEST OBSTACLE IS . . .

Ignorance.

AND . . .

Please. I'm forbidden to say.

SPEAK ITS NAME . . .

You must answer all the questions!

12

"Oh my god, Sam. You didn't tell me your dad's here," Jamie blurted out.

"Jamie, that wasn't me!" Sam whispered.

"What do mean, it wasn't you?"

"Someone else is in here!"

"Your dad's in *here*?"

"Not my dad! Someone else!"

Sam was pawing the wall for a switch, but it was crammed with shelves covered with equipment.

A glass beaker fell to the floor with a crash.

"Sam, if you're playing a joke on me, I will never forgive you — "

"Please . . . respond," the voice said in an odd monotone. "Dad, is that you?"

"Oh my god — it isn't you. It's different, isn't it?"

"Be cool, Jamie." Sam was shaking. "F-find the light switch."

"The . . . green light . . . at knee level . . . by the door," the voice said.

Sam saw it, but his arm froze.

He wasn't sure he wanted light.

What am I going to see?

Do I want to see it?

He backed toward the door. "Jamie? I think I changed my mind . . ."

"Here it is!"

Zzzzt.

The overhead fluorescent flickered on.

Sam's eyes shut. He braced himself, ready to bolt at a moment's notice.

Then, slowly, he peeked.

A table came into focus — large and round, made of solid black marble, with a dark wood cabinet underneath and a clear glass dome on top, a little larger than a basketball.

Inside the dome was what looked like an electronic honeycomb — four layers of motherboards, each crammed with cards of varying sizes. In front of the dome was an ordinary-looking keyboard and screen.

The table and the domed apparatus trailed nests of tangled wires. They snaked through the room, attached to various instruments along the wall.

And that was it.

No person at all.

"Where is he?" Jamie asked.

"HELP . . . ME!"

The voice was louder. It came from the center of the room.

And Sam noticed the screen for the first time:

>: PLEASE RESPOND. DAD, IS THAT YOU?

>: THE GREEN LIGHT AT KNEE LEVEL BY THE DOOR.

>: HELP ME.

They were the words that the computer had just spoken.

"I don't believe this . . ." Sam murmured.

Jamie looked from the dome to the screen. "This is Kevin?"

"HELLL — "

Sam ran his thumb along a thumbpad and double-clicked on DISABLE. The voice abruptly stopped.

"An alarm," Sam said.

"Kevin is an *alarm system?*"

"With my voice sampled into it."

"This is your twin?" Jamie hooted with laughter. "*This* was what you were afraid of?"

"I didn't know — "

" 'MAYbe a PART of him surVIVED,' " Jamie said, deepening her voice to a nerdy approximation of Sam's.

"I thought — "

" 'His BRAIN circuitry is incomPLETE!' "

"Knock it off, okay?" Sam slumped against a wall. He closed his eyes, half hoping he was in yet another nightmare.

It can't be just an alarm.

The system was too big. Too complex. It *had* to be something more important.

But what?

Jamie was clattering away at the keyboard. "This is so cool. I can disable the alarm . . . put it on 'Communication with Operator' . . . 'Voice Recognition' . . . guess that means I can talk to it, huh?"

"How should I know?"

"Hello!" Jamie shouted. "What is your name?"

"Kevin," the bubble responded.

KEVIN appeared on the monitor.

"Well, we were right about his name!" Jamie said to Sam, then turned back to the dome. "Yo, Kevin, what's up?"

"An adverb, as in 'stand up.' An adjective, as in 'the tent is up.' A preposition, as in 'she lives up the street.' A verb — "

Jamie laughed. "No, I mean, how are you feeling, my man?"

"Just fine, thank you. It is cold outside. The cold is seasonable. The humidity level is low. This combination fosters a feeling of comfort."

Sam cringed.

After all the years of late nights without Mom and Dad — after all the technotalk, the switches and neurotransmitters and circuits

— *this* is what they'd created? This was their life's work, the state of artificial intelligence?

This is what kept them away from me?

A talking computer that doubles as an alarm. And a machine that collects emotions but doesn't do anything with them.

These were impressive, in their own ways. But they weren't close to real brains.

Somehow Sam had expected more.

"So, Kev, what's the square root of one hundred fifty-seven?" Jamie asked.

"Twelve point five two nine nine six four," the monotonous voice replied.

My voice.

Sam could picture his parents deciding to make the machine sound like him. Then secretly taping him around the house to create voice samples. It would be their way of staying close to Sam while they were away from him. Creating a reminder.

That's what they wanted. A reminder of the son. Without any of the emotions and mess. Without the hassles of parenting.

So very, very *Hughes*.

They don't mean any harm, Sam.

That's just the way they are.

". . . And who was the seventh president of the United States?" Jamie asked.

"Andrew Jackson."

"Sam, this is amazing!" Jamie said with a grin. "It's a homework machine. Bart would love this. You could get him to pay you to come here."

Sam turned and opened the lab door. The hallway was empty. "Jamie, we have to go."

"Is someone here?"

"No, but what if this thing is connected to a central station? The police could be coming here right now!"

Jamie shot away from the machine, heading for the door. "See ya, Kevin. Thanks for the chat."

As she left, Sam glanced at the screen.

The voice had stopped, but words were scrolling across it anyway:

>: HI, KEVIN.

>: HI, DAD. WHAT DO YOU NEED?

>: I HAVE A CODE 4 HERE.

>: MISSING PERSON? WHO?

>: KEVIN, HAVE YOU SEEN SAM?

ITS NAME?

The . . . the Eleventh Force . . .

It's time. You must prepare.

I said the name.

It is all right. Soon you will not be here.

What if this doesn't work?

It may not.

Will I never return?

Perhaps.

13

Sam leaped back inside and pressed the POWER button.

The screen blinked off.

"What'd you do that for?" Jamie said.

"My dad's talking to it from his own computer."

"I thought you said he was sleeping!"

"He was, when I left. He must have gotten up!"

"So why'd you cut off the machine? What's your dad going to think when he gets no answer?"

With a loud beep, the bubble suddenly burst to life again.

"HELP! THIS SPACE HAS BEEN VIO-LATED!" the machine blared out.

Sam jumped. "What the — "

"Great, Sam. Just great — "

WOOOP! WOOOOP! WOOOOP!

The alarm echoed through the hallway, sharp and deafening. A flash of light caught Sam square in the eye.

Emergency lights. Glaring on and off from auxiliary spotlights along the wall.

Jamie and Sam bolted toward the stairwell at the end of the corridor.

But before the stairwell was an intersec-tion — and someone was in it.

More than one person. A cavalcade of foot-steps. Running toward them.

Where'd THEY come from?

Sam pulled Jamie back the way they'd come. They zoomed past Lab 6 again and darted into an empty hallway at the opposite end.

This path was clear. They headed toward an archway framed with garish red and white stripes. Around the stripes, a black-painted message warned DANGER: HAZARDOUS SUB-STANCES. AUTHORIZED PERSONNEL ONLY!

"WE CAN'T GO THERE!" Jamie shouted.

"Trust me," Sam said.

He remembered that the signs meant nothing. They scared away nosy visitors. Or spies.

The archway led to another corridor of small offices, which dead-ended at a metal door with even more warnings: DO NOT OPEN — FIRE ALARM WILL SOUND — NO ADMITTANCE.

The subbasement.

Mom and Dad called it "the catacombs."

Sam rammed his shoulder against the door.

"The alarm!" Jamie cried out.

"IT'S ALREADY SOUNDING!" Sam exclaimed.

The door smacked open. Just beyond it was a dark set of cement stairs lit by a single hanging lightbulb. The steps were littered with paint chips and plaster, the walls pocked and flaky.

"This is *down*!" Jamie shouted. "We need to go *out*!"

"Mom and Dad used to go down here all the time. For supplies. I think there's an exit on the other side."

"You *think*?"

Sam was already descending.

At the bottom, he swept away a dusty cobweb and looked into a long, low-ceilinged corridor. Tangled knots of plastic pipes crisscrossed overhead, some dropping to eye level. A narrow, rubble-strewn path lay between electronic equipment that had been shoved against the walls.

Sam jogged forward, hunched over. Down here, the alarm sounded muffled and distant. A mouse moved along a floor molding, quickly disappearing behind a pile of discarded monitors.

"Ow!" Jamie's voice sounded from behind him.

"Duck," Sam said.

"Thanks a lot."

Sam tried to envision where they were in relation to the floor above, but he had no idea.

They crossed a hallway, wider and less crowded than theirs. It sloped downward, ending at a large glass-paned door.

The faded lettering on the door read GENERATOR.

"There!" Sam shouted. "That's where the other exit is!"

He yanked the door open and ran in.

The room was cavernous. A walkway led around a large sunken area. In the middle was a gargantuan steel monster, droning steadily, its bottom covered by the darkness of a seemingly endless abyss.

At the other end of the walkway was the exit. Through the door, Sam hoped, was a stairway leading upward and eventually out of the building.

"You're a genius," said Jamie.

Sam sprinted across the walkway. The rickety wooden planks sagged beneath him.

He kept his eye on the frosted glass pane of the exit door. It was changing. He noticed a slight swelling of light. As if another door had opened, beyond and above it, at the top of the stairs.

Sam stopped. Now shadows were coming down the stairs toward him.

Trapped.

He and Jamie wouldn't make it to the other side. Not enough time.

"Now what?" Jamie whispered.

Sam spun around. Just behind them was a custodial closet, blocked by a broken brown table on wheels.

He pushed aside the table. His hand grazed a jagged shard of broken metal trim. It opened a deep scrape, but Sam ignored the pain and yanked open the door. Darting inside, he pulled Jamie in and shut the door behind them.

"I'm claustrophobic," Jamie whispered.

"I'm bleeding," Sam replied, pressing his hand against his shirt to stanch the flow.

SMMMACK!

The exit door slammed open against the inner wall of the generator room.

Sam tried to stay silent. But his and Jamie's breathing sounded like ungreased hacksaws.

Boots thudded on the walkway, just outside the closet.

"They're not here!" a voice called out.

"Keep going," cried another. "They're down here somewhere."

Yes. Keep going.

Yes.

"Someone check the closets," a third voice yelled.

"I will!"

Sam's breath caught in his throat.

"Bart," Jamie whispered.

"What's he doing here?" Sam whispered back.

"He must have seen me leave!"

"He *followed* us?"

"I don't know! Sam, what do we do n — "

"Ssshhh."

The corner. Crouch. Pull a bucket over your head.

Risky.

Stand still and hope they don't see you in the darkness.

Stupid.

Hit him with something.

Sam groped around for anything — a mop, a paint roller . . .

"Ow!" Jamie yelped, "that's my foot — "

Sam lost his balance. He fell against the back wall of the closet.

And the wall moved.

Farewell.

But the rest of the questions — are there no more questions?

This will have to do. You are fading.

14

Sam pushed again. A corner of the wall was swiveling on some kind of fulcrum. "Come on. There must be a room back here."

"I'm not going in there!" Jamie whispered.

TWHOCK-TWHOCK-TWHOCK-TWHOCK the approaching footsteps sounded.

Jamie leaned against the wall, hard.

It swung open, leaving a space just big enough for them to slip through. They entered a room of some kind, pitch-black and cold.

Sam and Jamie pushed the wall back. It

returned to its old position with a soft thump.

"There's blood on the knob!" Bart shouted. "They're in here."

Sam cringed. *Couldn't you have SEEN that metal edge, Hughes?*

Light entered through the thin crack where the swinging wall was hinged.

"HEY!" shouted Bart through the wall, inches away from them.

"Did you find them?" a more distant voice called.

Sam and Jamie heard Bart poking around, crashing against the wall, pulling things away.

THUMP.

The wall moved.

Jamie and Sam backed away.

"Ow," Bart exclaimed. "Nope. But one of them's bleeding. So keep an eye out for stains."

The closet door slammed shut, suddenly muffling the voices beyond it.

The footsteps receded into silence.

Gone.

"That fat, pinheaded tub of pork sushi — " Jamie muttered.

Sam let out a breath and slumped against the wall.

EEEP . . . EEEP . . . EEEP . . . EEEP . . .

Until that moment, Sam hadn't noticed the soft beeping noise behind him.

"Uh, let's get out of here," he said, feeling around for a handle.

Jamie joined him. "How do you pull this thing open?"

Sam's fingers brushed against a light switch.

He flicked it upward. Two overhead strips lit up.

The door handle was right in front of him. He clasped with his good hand and pulled.

The door was heavy. "Jamie, can you — "

But Jamie was standing rock-still, her back to the wall. Staring into the room.

Sam turned.

They were in a lab. Bigger than Lab 6 and windowless. Except for the area of the swivel door, the walls were covered floor to ceiling with electronic equipment. It felt like the inside of some high-tech submarine.

At the center was a table nearly obscured

by three rolling carts. On the table, under a black blanket, was a body.

"Oh my god . . ." Sam murmured.

"I . . . don't think we belong here," Jamie squeaked.

Sam moved close. "Is it alive?"

"ARE YOU CRAZY, SAM? GET AWAY FROM THAT!" She grabbed him by the arm, but Sam pulled away.

He couldn't take his eyes away from the inert silhouette.

Something about it was familiar.

"Sam?" Jamie's voice was tense, sharp. "It's a dead body. If you touch it — if you get your fingerprints on it and someone finds it — I will say I never met you."

Its chest was not moving. But it didn't smell like a dead body. Dead bodies were supposed to smell, weren't they?

Sam stood over the figure and pulled back the black cloth.

He gagged.

Jamie screamed.

A face stared back at Sam. A face he knew well.

His own.

15

*H*e did exist.
He was here, all this time.
In some kind of coma.
Just the way Jamie said.
BUT FOR FOURTEEN YEARS?
How?
How could it have happened? How could he have survived?
How could I not have found out?
WHY DIDN'T THEY TELL ME?
Sam felt detached, dizzy. He grabbed the

side of the table. His fingers brushed against Kevin's cheek.

It was cold. And smooth.

Silky smooth.

Sam pulled his arm back.

"Sam, what is going on?" Jamie asked. "Is he alive?"

"No," Sam said.

"HE'S DEAD?"

"No."

"WELL, THEN WHAT IS HE?"

Sam placed his hand on the cheek again. He scratched the skin with his fingernail. Deep.

It ripped cleanly. No blood.

BEEEEP-BEEEEP-BEEEEP!

On one of the rolling tables a monitor blinked with the words INITIATE EPITHELIAL SEALANT.

Epithelial — that was one of the words he'd seen on his dad's computer. Sam knew that word. From biology.

It meant *of or relating to the upper layer of skin*. Something like that.

The cheek was epithelial, all right. It was

just like skin. But it wasn't skin. It was synthetic. It needed "sealant."

"He's . . . not a he," Sam said.

"What does THAT mean?"

"He's an *it* . . ."

"Sam, this is too weird. We don't belong here, Sam — "

"He's — "

Kevin.

No. Not Kevin. How could this be Kevin? This was just a *copy*. A humanoid. A model of how Kevin would have looked had he lived.

Another of Mom and Dad's secret projects.

A lifelike reconstruction of someone that never existed.

The kid I "absorbed."

Why? What was the point?

To admire him? To pretend he was alive? To dream about what might have been?

It was sad.

It was sick.

Sam heard a new commotion. Above them. He instinctively looked up, but his head hurt too much.

The lights around him flashed and blurred.

A thousand instruments, all waiting for something.

And then it hit him.

It suddenly made sense.

The body needs a brain.

The brain needs a soul.

The body is on the table.

The soul is in me. Crowding me.

But I can pass it on.

Into the transpatheter.

Which loads it into the brain.

And then —

KEVIN.

"No!" Sam cried out, clutching his head.

The voice was back. The *feeling* was back.

But — how — ?

"SAM!"

Jamie reached out to help him. Something was happening but Sam couldn't focus, couldn't pay attention, couldn't move.

Sam sank to his knees. The other voice inside him was louder and more agitated than before *(WHY ARE YOU DOING THIS TO ME? THIS WILL KILL YOU)* — and Sam didn't know what it meant so he tried to talk to it mentally *(Who are you? Are you Kevin?)*

146

but the voice was growing louder, deafening, stretching Sam's mind until he thought his head was about to blow apart. *(IT'S NOT GOING TO WORK! IT'S NOT MEANT TO BE!)*

"What?" Sam said aloud, his voice strangled and weak. "WHAT'S not going to work?"

"Sam!" Jamie was pulling him up now. "They're coming!"

They?

Who?

"HELLLP . . . ME!" The words came out of Sam's mouth — but they weren't from *him*. The other voice — the other person — was speaking through Sam now.

"What do you want?" Sam answered.

Jamie thought he was talking to her. "To get you out of here!"

"YES . . . GET ME . . . OUT OF HERE!" cried the voice.

"I'm trying to!" Jamie urged. "Come on!"

"Why are you back, Kevin?" Sam pleaded. "I thought I lost you in the transpatheter!"

Jamie looked at him, horrified. "Sam, who are you talking to?"

She loosened her grip. Sam fell back.

147

His head hit the floor.

"Let me go," the voice spoke through Sam, softer now. Reassuring. "You'll be all right."

Jamie was still pulling at him. "I can't let you go, Sam."

"Let me go."

Yes.

Do it, Sam.

Have some peace.

Finally.

But how?

What was Kevin asking? Was he asking to die?

How do I do it?

How does one person die inside another?

As Sam's eyes closed, he realized.

He knew.

He had taken Kevin's life.

Now Kevin was getting revenge.

Absorbing him back.

A life for a life.

Jamie yelled.

The wall swung open.

But Sam didn't hear either sound.

CHANGE OF WATCHER STATUS

Completion: Unknown

16

When the explosion happened, Sam was rising.

The light above him was pure, cold, and white.

Into the light.

Death. The way people describe it.

A scream resounded in the room, blotting out all sound. It was his own voice — but he was outside it somehow, listening. Floating in the light. Hovering. Bodiless. Sightless.

He was pure energy now.

And he knew what had happened, even though he couldn't see it.

His brain had split.

But there were no pieces. No grisly aftermath.

It had divided like a cell.

Two minds. Equal, whole, and separate.

Kevin's voice was fading away. But it no longer pleaded. Instead, it babbled on about nonsense — superstrings and parallel this-and-that, the same words over and over, like a chant.

Sam was aware of time passing — a great deal of time. But the length was meaningless. An hour in a nanosecond. He heard other voices around him, too, not just Kevin's. Frantic and familiar. Mom. Dad. Jamie.

Where are they?

He wanted to see them. More than anything else.

He struggled to see.

Eyes — I must have eyes.

And the pain surged back in.

Unspeakable pain that went beyond screaming, that exhausted more than hurt.

He realized he was no longer floating.

He was lying on his back, and he could feel again.

His head was covered. It prickled, warm and uncomfortable. His joints were stiff, as if he'd been asleep for days. And his cheek hurt.

As he opened his eyes, the images around him seemed blotchy and pixilated, the colors too bright and harsh.

His mom and dad drew closer around him.

"Mm . . . daaaa." His tongue felt thick, his jaw stiff.

Now Jamie came into sight. Her eyes were wide as softballs, her mouth open in shock.

What? What's happened to me?

He tried to sit but his arms and legs were tied down. He realized he was wearing the transpatheter helmet.

All he could move was his head.

Craning his neck, he saw the body lying on the table next to him. It, too, was wearing a transpatheter helmet.

Kevin.

I was right. They must have "activated" the body. Transferred Kevin out of me and into it.

"Ih wwooo."

Mom's face was streaked with tears. "What's he saying?"

Sam struggled to repeat himself, moving his mouth slowly like an infant learning to speak for the first time. "It . . . wworrrked. The brrrraaain . . . innn Laab Six — "

"Yes, Sam, it worked," Mr. Hughes said.

"Yyyou put it . . . innnto the bo-o-ody," Sam said. "Ssssu-u-urgicalllly. While I wa-a-as ssssleeping."

"Yes," Mrs. Hughes replied.

"Bu-u-ut it isn't a brrrain, is it?"

Mrs. Hughes shook her head. "Not without the transpatheter."

"The three had to work together — the body, the brain, the transpatheter. We weren't expecting to have to do it so soon. We thought, maybe another month . . ."

It was all becoming clear now.

I absorbed him, all right. And he stayed with me.

His essence.

He grew as I grew — hidden away in some corner of my brain, some part of the unused eighty-five percent.

But he awakened whenever I was near Turing-Douglas.

Whenever I was near the transpatheter.

That was his escape. He could sense it. The way a dog becomes agitated when he knows a visitor's near.

That was why he took over my dreams — Dad had brought a transpatheter into the house. Kevin was sending me hints. Warning me not to do this.

But why?

Sam knew he wouldn't have all the answers for a long time.

But he felt grateful.

They've completed the task. So he's been transferred. Into the —

The —

Something was wrong.

Way wrong.

Everyone had turned to the android.

It was sitting up.

Sam's vision was still blotchy. But he could see that the android was wearing the clothes *he'd* been wearing. And the table it was lying on was brown, not black.

It was the table that had been out in the hall.

On its hand, a bright red scab had formed.

"I did it," it said.

"Yes, Sam," Jamie told it. "You did it."

No.

NO!

Sam swung his forearm up to feel his face.

The cut on his cheek was clean and blood-less.

WATCHERS

Case File: 7222

Name: Samuel Hughes

Age: 13

First contact: 41.33.02

Acceptance: Suspended

Marion Ettlinger

ABOUT THE AUTHOR

Peter Lerangis is the author of many popular books, including two young-adult thrillers (*The Yearbook* and *Driver's Dead*) and four middle-grade novels (*Spring Fever, Spring Break, It Came from the Cafeteria,* and *Attack of the Killer Potatoes*). Mr. Lerangis lives in New York City with his wife, Tina deVaron, and their two sons, Nick and Joe. Read more about Watchers in KIDS' BOOKS at www.scholastic.com (www.scholastic.com/tradebks/watchers).

Meet the Guardians
of the Force.

STAR WARS®

JEDI APPRENTICE

☐ BDN51922-0 #1: The Rising Force
☐ BDN51925-5 #2: The Dark Rival
☐ BDN51933-6 #3: The Hidden Past

$4.99 Each!